HOT FOR SANTA

A STEAMY HOLIDAY SHORT STORY

MELANIE A. SMITH

WICKED DREAMS PUBLISHING

Tough Love

Finding His Redemption

Short Stories

Cruising for Love

Hot for Santa

Anthologies

Heroes With Heat and Heart 2: A Charity Anthology

HOT FOR SANTA

Whoever invented holiday parties can kiss my big, fat ass. I mean really, they're just a recipe for disaster. Well, at least for me. Socially awkward introvert? Check. Enough alcohol to make me say something irrevocably embarrassing? Check. My ridiculously hot boss who I've had a crush on since I started working here seven years ago dressed as the sexiest Santa I've ever seen? Check.

Well, sort of. I mean, it's just a regular Santa suit. But holy hell. I know what I'll be dreaming about tonight.

Unfortunately, I don't have much of a choice but to sit here, pretending to enjoy my spiked eggnog and making small talk with my coworkers. I can only hope like hell that they don't notice me stealing glances at Logan every chance I get.

He wasn't my boss when I started. He was just another engineer working alongside me, though he was already on his way up, being ten years my senior. He only became my boss last year, and it's been a constant battle not to ogle him daily. He's the epitome of the silver fox, though he's only in his mid-forties. I mean, I went gray early too, but I don't think there's a female equivalent. So even though I'm only thirty-five, hair dye is a must. But he pulls it off. The well-tailored clothes he usually wears that accent his tall, lean, athletic frame don't hurt the sexy-older-man image either. But I'm completely in the friend zone, having only become close with him platonically over the years we've worked together.

And it might be the rum, but I suddenly can't help wishing I was brave enough to make a move. Or really, that I'd been brave enough back when he wasn't my boss. Not that he's ever shown any particular interest beyond friend-ship, even if I am tempted to take his attentions the wrong way from time to time. Until I remind myself that he's just a sweetheart to everyone. But it hasn't stopped me from obsessing over him all these years, despite myself.

My eyes roam the large conference room, packed with the few dozen people on our team, decorated to the hilt with garland and red ribbons, the table in the center of the room piled high with cookies, drinks, and candy. But my eyes always find him. Right now, he's talking to my lead by the door, his face lit up with a smile that gets me every damn time.

"Earth to Evie." A hand waves in front of my face.

"Hmmm?" I murmur. My eyes refocus on Elaine, who is standing in front of me with a look of exasperation.

"What are you staring at?" she asks curiously, looking over her shoulder. Thankfully, Logan had just vacated the spot he'd been standing in.

"Nothing, just zoning out," I reply, kicking myself for almost getting caught. "I'm so ready for the break." Just another short stretch of pretending to enjoy socializing and forced merry-making and I get a whole week off to do … well, not a whole hell of a lot. I don't really go anywhere for the holidays. But hey, it's a week off.

"Me too," she agrees. "I'm just glad we got that testing done under the wire. Otherwise, Logan would probably have made us stay here all weekend."

Her words make me freeze on the spot. Because we did get the testing done. And I even finished my report this morning. Or I thought I did, until Elaine's comment made me realize I forgot to include the wiring diagrams.

"Shit," I curse quietly under my breath.

"Everything okay?"

I shake my head. "No. My report wasn't complete. But it'll only take me an hour or two to fix it. I should go."

She crosses her arms over her chest and gives me a

skeptical look. "Really? Or did you just forget to bring a secret Santa gift?"

My jaw drops, realizing I had, in fact, forgotten that too. Thankfully I'm saved by Logan coming back in the room with the huge red bag that had been living in his office, collecting gifts.

"Time for presents!" he declares over the din. Elaine even forgets me, migrating with him through the room. With her diverted, and since there's not a present in there from me anyway, I decide now's a pretty damn good time to sneak away. So, as he settles the bag on a chair at the opposite end of the conference room, I make my escape.

As soon as I'm out of the crowded room, I breathe a sigh of relief and chuck my half-full eggnog cup in the nearest garbage can. I'm usually not this forgetful, but this is one instance where I'm happy to have forgotten just so I have an excuse to bail out of the party early. Even if it does mean I'll end up working late.

ALMOST TWO HOURS LATER, I LEAN BACK IN MY CHAIR AND stretch widely. It's not perfect, but it's good enough. I upload the revision to the network and reply all to my original email letting everyone know the report has been updated. I doubt anyone but Logan will look at it until we're back from the holidays, but they can't say I didn't finish it before the break.

I close up shop and lock my laptop away, determined to take a real break this week. I love my job, but even I can admit I probably work a little too much. I plan to really sink into laziness for a full nine days over the next two weekends and week between, only emerging to do the mandatory Christmas brunch with my parents. Otherwise, it'll be lots of reading, watching TV, and sleeping in. I imagine for most people that sounds like heaven. Don't get me wrong, I'm looking forward to decompressing, but I'm going to have to force myself to relax every step of the way. Weird, I know. But it's not for no good reason I haven't gotten married, had kids, and all that. Work has been my main focus, by choice.

I grab my purse and my gym bag and head out. As I make it out of the cubicle farm and walk past the offices, I notice Logan's light is still on. I'm a little surprised, since I heard the party break up and everyone head out a bit ago. And Logan's big on leading by example to show his team that "life-work" balance, as he calls it, is important. Though I know for a fact he still takes his laptop home and works nights and weekends. Still, I understand why he tries to get everybody else to have a life. Not everyone is wired to work as much as we do.

"Evie?" he calls as I walk past. I'd hoped to sneak by unnoticed, but obviously no such luck today.

I back up a few steps until I'm standing in his doorway. He's still wearing the Santa suit, though the hat now sits on the couch to the right side of his office. Lord help me.

"Santa?" I ask teasingly.

He looks up from his laptop with a grin. "Come in and close the door," he instructs.

I raise an eyebrow, but do as he asks, putting my bags down and settling in a chair across from him. "What's up?"

He closes his laptop, shoves it to the side, and leans back in his chair. "I saw your email. Thanks for staying to take care of that."

I shrug, unsure of why that needed to be said behind closed doors. "Of course. You know me, I hate loose ends."

"I do. Which is why I asked you to close the door. Because even though everyone's probably already gone, I don't want to chance it."

"I … don't understand," I admit.

He leans forward on his arms, knitting his fingers together. "I did a quick review of everyone's reports this morning before the party. Unfortunately, Randy's portion was … let's call it a bit of a mess. I can't send it to our client in its current state."

I press my lips together to keep myself from saying anything negative. But I don't think I need to; it's an unspoken understanding that Randy, one of our newest hires, already isn't our best performer. In fact, he's been on notice for exactly that a couple of times, though always managing to shape up just enough to not get canned.

"I see. And you want my help bringing it up to snuff, I take it?"

"I hate to ask given that we're all supposed to be taking some much-needed time off, but yes, I do. If you're willing." The pleading look he gives me alone would make me say yes. I don't think I'm wired to deny him anything. Even without the crush, he's a good friend and an even better boss, always going the extra mile for his team. How could I possibly say no?

"You know I've always got your back, Logan."

He breathes a sigh of relief. "One of the many things I love about you, Evie."

My heart skips a beat, and I try not to show how flustered I am. He blushes suddenly, clearly realizing that was probably an odd thing to say.

"Send it to me. I'll look at it after dinner and let you know how long I think it'll take. Hopefully we can get it done before we're too far out of deadline."

"Thanks," he says, letting out a relieved sigh. "I tried to talk them out of a pre-holiday deadline for exactly this reason, but you know how that goes."

I gather my things and rise, already making a mental

checklist of all the things I'll need to bring home to make sure I can get this done as soon as possible.

"I do," I agree distractedly, grabbing the door handle. "Talk to you soon?"

He nods as I twist the door handle. But nothing happens.

He steps around his desk. "Sorry, that thing's been acting weird. Sometimes you have to jiggle it."

I give it a try, but it still doesn't open, so I pull harder. "Man, this thing's really —" Suddenly I'm flying backward with part of the handle clasped in my fist. I knock backward into Logan, and he nimbly catches me before I fall to the ground.

"Oh my god, are you okay?" he asks, helping me back to my feet.

I can feel my face flushed bright red. "I'm fine," I murmur, horribly embarrassed. "But I think I might've broken your doorknob."

I hold up the handle and we both look back at the door. The round part is still attached, now with a jagged edge where the aluminum handle bent and snapped off.

Logan bursts out laughing and, though I didn't think it possible, my mortification deepens.

"Damn, Evie, I had no idea you were so strong," he teases, going to the door to try to open it. The smile melts off his face. "Uhhh…" He grips the round part on the undamaged side, but it clearly won't budge at all anymore.

"Oh my god, I really, really broke it," I whisper.

Logan turns away from the door, scanning his office. He takes a pair of scissors out of the organizer on his desk and has a go at the hinges. But those won't budge either, despite his working at it for a few minutes.

"Damn, I think these are painted in," he mutters. He sets the scissors aside and squats under the handle, examining the smooth plate around it. "No visible screws or obvious ways to take this apart." He stands back up and tries to use the scissors to separate the plate from the door, also to no avail.

"I'm so sorry, Logan," I say, covering my eyes with my hands.

I feel his large, warm hands close around my wrists, tugging my hands away from my eyes. I look up into his hazel eyes to find them warmed by the smile he's giving me. "Hey, it's fine. I'll call maintenance and we'll be out of here in no time," he assures me.

He places the call and I listen to his side of the conversation. Which doesn't go well. Turns out maintenance is also gone for the holidays. They will try to get someone back in, but if nothing else, the cleaners will be here in a few hours and can help.

"A few *hours*?" I gasp after he's hung up.

"I'm sorry, Evie, I should've had that damn thing fixed ages ago," he replies, running a hand through his hair.

I chew on my lip, trying not to freak out. Why? Because I'm very careful not to be alone with Logan for five minutes, much less for hours. There's no telling what awkward confession might spill out, and he's my boss now.

"Is there anyone else we can call? Maybe someone on our team can come back in and try to help?" I ask.

"That's … not exactly something I can ask people to do," he hedges.

"Shit, I'm sorry, I totally get it. You're their boss. It'd be weird."

"Just a little. You could though, if you feel like you're on close enough terms with any of them to make that kind of request," he offers.

I shake my head. "I'm not. I don't even have anyone else's personal number," I admit. I chew on my lip as we stare at each other. The building requires a badge to enter, so it's not exactly like there's anyone else we can get to help us.

"Maybe we should take the opportunity to work on the report?" he suggests.

"Do you have access to the lab data collection program?"

He purses his lips. "No, I don't."

"Then there's not much I can do from here."

Logan saunters over to his couch, sinking onto it resignedly. "Well, then I guess we wait." He pats the cushion next to him. "Which is great, because I've always wanted to know your life story," he teases.

With a reticent smirk, I take a seat next to him, putting my bags down next to me and perching gingerly on the edge of the couch. I pull at the ends of my dark brown hair.

"Really?" I ask, half teasing, half truly wondering.

He flashes me a grin and leans in a little. "Would you be surprised if I said yes?"

My eyes go wide, but I'm saved responding when the phone on his desk rings. He rises and answers. And it's obviously the maintenance contact, but he simply listens without any expression. When he hangs up, he turns back to me, shaking his head.

"The maintenance guy is already on an airplane to Florida and his backup isn't answering. The cleaning crew might be able to come in a little earlier, but not much as they've got another job before us."

"So, we're stuck here."

He sits back down next to me, shifting uncomfortably. "We're stuck here," he confirms.

I point to his hand, which is now scratching under his collar.

"Everything okay there, Mr. Claus?"

He huffs a laugh. "Nobody ever tells you being Santa is

itchy as hell," he replies. "But then…" He trails off, giving me a nervous look.

"What?"

He shakes his head, ducking his chin. I dip down to look at him and he's *blushing*.

"God, now I'm really curious," I admit with a laugh.

"I can't tell you, of all people," he mutters. I don't think I've ever seen him this embarrassed, and for some reason it's making me giddy. Maybe because *I* always feel like I'm embarrassing myself around him.

"Me, of all people?"

"Yes," he says firmly, lifting his chin, though he's still fire-engine red. Or maybe, Santa Claus red. The thought makes me laugh even harder. "I'm glad my misery is amusing." Thankfully he sounds like he's joking, but I try hard and finally get control of myself.

"I'm sorry, I've just never seen you look so uncomfortable."

"Fine. If you must know…" He pauses, then shakes his head. "No, I can't." He stands up, then throws himself dramatically back into his desk chair.

"Give me a little hint," I beg, tears of laughter in my eyes.

He sighs heavily. "Fine. Here's your hint: I lost a bet."

"Oooh interesting. To who?"

He shoots me a wary look. "One of the other managers.

Who shall remain nameless in case this blows up in my face like I think it's about to."

"Is that why you're dressed as Santa? I mean, you've always been into the holiday party, but I think this is the first time you've done that."

He rolls his eyes. "Yes, that's why I'm dressed as Santa. *Only* as Santa." He gives me a meaningful look and I gasp in understanding.

"Oh my god, Logan, are you naked under that suit?"

He turns flaming red this time and buries his face in his hands. "Yes," he groans.

I laugh so loud and so hard that I'm crying and in danger of peeing my pants. When I finally gather myself, wiping the tears from my eyes, he's shooting me stink-eye from his chair.

"Oh man," I sigh as the last few titters escape me. "Well, I can understand why you'd be so itchy. What is that, polyester?"

"I think it's rayon, actually," he grumbles.

Another laugh threatens to burst out of me, but I put my hand over my mouth.

"Don't you have a change of clothes?"

"No. I was about to go home when you walked by." He scratches at his neck again.

"Wait a minute," I say, holding up a finger. I pick up my gym bag and rummage through it, extracting an oversized T-shirt I use to work out in. "Try this on. It's clean."

He holds the plain, white shirt up, eyeing it for size. "You sure?" he asks.

"I'm sure. I wouldn't want you scratching yourself raw over the next few hours," I reply drily.

"Well, thanks," he replies.

"Sure. I hope it fits, anyway."

"I'm sure it will." His eyes flick down to my chest and my eyebrows shoot up. I'm busty, so I'm used to men staring at my breasts. But *he's* never looked before. His eyes jump back to mine and he clears his throat. "I mean, it's better than nothing."

I stare back at him, tension crackling in the air.

"Ahh, Evie?" he raises his eyebrows, and I realize he's asking me to give him privacy.

"Oh, geez, sorry, of course." I blush fiercely and turn away so he can change.

A few swishing sounds of fabric later, he tells me he's done. When I turn back around, my jaw almost drops in shock. It fits him like a second skin, highlighting every muscle in his chest, abs, and upper arms. The sight is distracting, to say the least, and something inside me aches to touch him. I swallow hard and work to move my eyes up to meet his.

"Looks good." My voice comes out in an embarrassing squeak, and I want to crawl in a hole and die.

He gives me a knowing smirk. "It'll do. Thank you."

I nod and avert my eyes, not trusting myself to keep looking him in the eye or say anything else without drooling. And wondering why the hell the universe is testing me like this.

I hear him stand, then feel the weight of him settling back on the couch next to me.

"Since we're going to be here a while, why don't you tell me why you haven't pushed for a promotion in the last few years."

I scrunch my brows together. "I'm a level four. Any higher and I'd have to become a manager or a technical lead."

He gives a small shrug. "So, why don't you?"

I give one in return. "I'm happy where I am. Is that so bad?"

He considers me for a moment. "I guess not. But I think you'd make an excellent technical lead, for what it's worth."

"Thanks, but then I'd have to rely on the cooperation of all the other technical leads that are men twenty-plus years older than me. They already give me a hard enough time."

"Evie, please. Most of our good-ol'-boy technical leads are

horrible with people too. But the opposite — they don't always understand or get along well with people your age, exactly like you just said. Frankly, I think it's a space that's begging to be filled. You could bridge a lot of gaps in that role."

"I'd have to represent the department. Give presentations."

His brow furrows. "And?"

I look up and press my lips together, trying to decide how to admit this. When I look back at him, he's studying me closely with those sharp eyes of his. And it makes me uncomfortable on a whole other level. I work hard to focus on what I want to say.

"I think we both know I'm hopelessly awkward. I wouldn't want to embarrass you in front of your peers." I can feel the blush rising, but I hold his gaze, determined not to surrender to my feelings of inadequacy. Both for the role and for catching the attention of someone like him.

Logan uncrosses his legs and sits upright, his eyes searching mine intently.

"Is that really how you see yourself?"

"I — yes. Isn't that how everyone sees me?"

"Wow." He stands up and paces the floor for a minute, ending up standing behind his desk. He runs a hand over the stubble on his chin. "I'm going to try to say this in the most appropriate way possible. But ... damn, Evie." He shakes his head and puts his hands on his hips. The way his muscles tense under the tight shirt as he considers me is getting more and more distracting. "You are incredibly smart and hard-working. And yes, you're a little adorably awkward, but it only adds to your charm. You are *more* than qualified to be a technical lead."

My heart flutters in my chest, and I look up at him in disbelief. "You … think I'm adorable?"

"*Adorably awkward*," he says, emphasizing each word with his hands.

"And charming."

"Okay, now it's just plain awkward." He rubs the back of his neck with a sheepish grin.

"I wish you wouldn't say things like that," I reply with a sigh, rubbing my eyes with my knuckles.

I feel him settle back next to me. "I'm sorry. We've been friends for a long time now. But you're right. As your boss, it was totally inappropriate."

I look up at him. "That's not what I meant," I whisper.

His eyes drop to my lips and hope twists to a staccato beat in my heart. "What did you mean?"

Now my heart starts pounding furiously as I consider giving him a real answer. I've never been a risk-taker, but then … when will I ever have an opportunity like this again? And I realize I kind of need to tell him. Because maybe, just maybe it'll help me stop pining for him.

"I *like* you, Logan. More than I should. I have for a

long time. You shouldn't say things like that because I'll take it the wrong way. Even though I know you're a good guy and you're just being nice to me. But it's not going to help me to stop liking you."

He stares at me, wide-eyed and speechless.

"I'm sorry. I just made it even more awkward. If you want to go work at your desk and pretend like I'm not here for the next couple of hours, I totally understand."

Slowly, he shakes his head, and his eyes focus again. His gaze locks on mine.

"Do you remember your first day, when we all went out for drinks at the end of the day?" he asks.

"Like it was yesterday," I reply. Because it's when I started falling for him. Watching him interact with easy grace, laughing, being the life of the party. He was everything I wished I could be. Confident, smart, and easy to get along with. And he was so, so sexy. Still is. Even in a white T-shirt and Santa pants. Maybe even more so. But all that, I don't say. It's bad enough I said as much as I did, and I can only hope whatever he's about to say doesn't crush me too badly.

"Your hair was in this librarian-style bun thing," he says, reaching out and rifling his fingers through the ends of my hair, causing me to freeze in place. "You had on this super-serious little black suit. And you were so *quiet*. I thought maybe if I was loud enough, you'd notice me over all the other guys trying to get your attention."

My breath catches in my throat and tears sting the backs of my eyes at the tenderness in his voice. "Why didn't you say anything?"

He gives me a vague smile, withdrawing his hand. "By the time I worked up the courage, you were dating someone else."

My eyebrows scrunch together. "I didn't start dating anyone until *months* after I'd started here. And we've known each other for seven years—"

"I know," he interrupts. "It's no excuse. I was a chicken-shit. But here you are, being adorably awkward and far braver than I ever could be when it came to you."

A frown tugs at my lips. "I find this all really hard to believe."

He chuckles tolerantly. "You really don't see yourself the way others do."

"Guess not."

Logan presses his lips together and gives me a long look. "You don't really share much about yourself, Evie, and you're kind of intimidatingly smart and beautiful. I'm also not a pushy guy. After a while I didn't know if you were still involved or what. I've only gotten to know you as well as I do by taking the small bits you were willing to give over the years. But I told myself to stop thinking about you that way a long time ago."

"And did you?"

"Not even a little." After a beat of silence, he speaks again. "Why now?"

"What do you mean?" I ask.

"I mean, why did you wait until now to tell me? If you've really been interested all this time."

I work my fingers together nervously, not quite sure how to respond.

"It's the Santa suit, isn't it?" he teases, trying to lighten the mood. "You've got a Santa fetish and it pushed you over the edge."

I laugh and shove him lightly. I want to deny it, but I'd be hard pressed to pretend like seeing him in the suit didn't do anything for me. Especially once I knew he was naked under it. That particular thought sends a shiver through me.

"I don't know," I finally admit. "Maybe I was tired of feeling this way. Maybe it's just time for me to move on, and telling you was the final step to getting it out of my system. I mean, if it was going to happen, it would've, right?"

He looks at me like I've grown a second head. "You do realize I basically just told you I'd never stopped thinking about you that way?"

I cock my head. "I … guess I missed that part."

He shakes his head and laughs. "Adorably awkward *and* a little dense," he teases.

"But you're my boss now."

"I am."

"And it would probably be a bad idea to date one of your direct reports."

"Yes, I suppose it would."

"So, this doesn't change anything."

"No." His hazel eyes darken with intensity as he leans into me, bringing his hand to my cheek. "It changes everything, Evie." As his thumb strokes my cheek, I realize it's the most contact we've had in years. By design, because even small touches have served to remind me how much he affects me. I'm reminded forcefully of that when everything in me lights up and I lean into his touch. I look up at him from under my lashes, unsure of what to do or say.

"It doesn't have to. I don't want to do anything that could get you in trouble. We don't have to cross this line," I insist. And even as I hear the words coming out of my mouth, my head is screaming, *What the hell is wrong with you?*

"I'm not making that mistake again," he says with a cluck of his tongue.

"What mistake?"

"Letting you slip through my fingers." He brings his other hand to my face, gently stroking his thumbs over my jaw. "Say yes, Evie. Say yes and I'll switch to another damn department if that's what it takes to be with you."

My heart twists, this time in a good way. And there's only one answer I can give.

"Yes," I whisper.

I move to meet him just as he lowers his face to mine, and our lips meet. Soft and slow at first, then firm and demanding as I allow myself to sink into him. It's so much more than I ever could've imagined. It's sweetness, and passion, and a desire so deep that there isn't a part of me that doesn't ache for him.

When he pulls away, I sigh. Out of satisfaction or longing, I don't know which. Maybe both.

"Now I wish I'd said something sooner."

Logan chuckles. "In a way, me too. But in another way, I think things happen when they're meant to. Even if I am wearing ridiculous pants and a woman's shirt right now."

I reach out, placing a hand on his chest, then running it up and over his shoulder. "If you don't like it, you can give it back," I tell him with a wink.

He tilts his head and gives me a look of pure desire. "You're lucky we could have company at any moment. I've been waiting a long time to hear something like that come out of your mouth."

"It's going to take me a while to wrap my head around that," I admit.

"Me too," he agrees. "But I think it would help if we kept doing this…" And his lips are back on mine, this time with his hands pulling me into his lap. I squeal against his mouth and wrap my arms around his neck, allowing him to gather me to him. And it feels so damn good to be in his arms.

Screw the Santa dreams later; right now, kissing him, knowing he's wanted me as much a I've wanted him is better than anything I have or could ever dream.

But when there's a loud knock on the door, we spring apart.

"Logan?" Katie's voice calls through the door. "Are you still here?"

Logan jumps up and grabs his Santa jacket, pulling it back on quickly while I straighten my clothes.

"I am, but the door handle is—" The door pops open and Katie peers inside, looking puzzled. "—broken. Well, thank you for liberating us."

Katie's eyes fall on me, and I do my best not to look like I've just been making out with our boss.

"Seems okay to me," she says suspiciously.

Logan points to the inside of the doorknob. "Evie hulked out on it. We've been stuck in here waiting for the cleaning crew to rescue us," he explains.

I shoot him a dirty look. "I did *not* 'hulk out,'" I scoff. "It was broken before I got here."

Logan holds his hands up in surrender. "She's right. I confess."

Katie looks at the busted doorknob and shrugs.

"Have you been in the building this whole time?" I ask her, realizing we never thought to try calling people at their desks.

"No," she replies, letting the door swing all the way open. "I left my wallet in my desk, so I came back for it." She looks between Logan and I, and I can't tell if her expression is suspicious or concerned. "Everything okay?"

"Yup," I assure her, rising and grabbing my bags. "I just need to go back and get my laptop. Turns out the reports need some polishing. We'd just finished discussing it when I 'hulked out.'" I shoot Logan another dirty look.

He shoots me a wry smirk in return. Katie seems satisfied, though, which is good. We almost blew it before we'd even really started.

"Okay, well, hope you guys have a good break." With that, she turns and heads out.

Logan and I exchange relieved glances.

"I'm going to get my things," I say softly.

He nods. "I'll wait here and walk you out."

I bite my bottom lip to suppress a smile and hoof it to my office. I meet back up with Logan and he walks me to my car in the parking garage. At this point it's clear we are the only two left, as ours are the only cars in sight. I toss everything in the backseat and turn back to find Logan staring at me, still looking incredibly hot in his Santa suit.

I grab hold of the white faux-fur lining on the lapels and pull him toward me. "I bet you can't wait to get out of this."

He looks down at me, one eyebrow raised. "Is that an offer to help?" he teases.

I blush hard and look down. "I don't know. Maybe. You make a pretty sexy Santa, Logan."

He hooks a finger under my chin, tilting my face up to look into his.

"I'll have to keep the suit for a while longer, then. But first, I want to take you on a date. Well, a lot of dates, actually. If that's okay with you?"

"More than okay."

A slow smile creeps over his face. "Good." He pulls me to him, his lips capturing mine in another toe-curling kiss that promises many others. And so much more. When he lets me go, I'm breathless, my hands settled on the warm, hard muscles of his chest. "I'd wish you a happy holiday, but I'm hoping to see you a whole hell of a lot sooner than that."

I can't help grinning up at him. "I hope so too."

"Then we'll call this goodbye, for a little while."

"A very little while?"

"That depends. What are you doing tonight?"

"You mean besides the report?"

He leans his forehead against mine and groans. "Damn. Tomorrow?"

"How about I call you as soon as the report is finished?"

"You'd better." His hands slide around me, pulling me in as close as possible. "Why do I feel like if I let you go now this will all have been a dream?"

I hold him tightly, burying my face in his chest. "I know how you feel." I tilt my head up to look at him. "If it makes you feel better, I'm probably not going to sleep until the damn report is done."

Logan chuckles, and it reverberates into me through our connected bodies. It feels good to be so close to him after all this time. Seven years of wanting each other. Of miscommunication and missed opportunities. But no more.

"It does make me feel better," he admits.

"Good. Because you'll see me again before you know it."

It takes a long time, and a lot more kissing, before we're able to part. And the whole drive home, I have a ridiculous grin that I can't wipe off my face.

The idea of seeing him as soon as I'm done with the report is quite possibly the best motivation I've ever had, and I finish the report in less than three hours while I scarf down dinner. So it's not even ten o'clock when I call Logan to let him know it's done.

Ten minutes later, there's a knock on the door. I open it to Logan. Still in the Santa suit.

"Did you even look at the report?" I tease, stepping back to let him in.

"I'll look at it tomorrow," he assures me, not taking his eyes off me. He extends an arm and offers me a small pile of white fabric. "Here's your shirt back. Thanks for the loan."

I take it from him with a raised eyebrow as I close the door behind him. "So, what are you wearing under the Santa jacket, then?"

Logan advances on me, backing me against the door. "Nothing," he replies. Chills run the entire length of my body. "And I know I said dates first, but that was before I had a few hours for reality to catch up with me." He runs a thumb over my lips, staring down at me ravenously.

"Well, we're not at work anymore. There's nothing stopping us."

His nose dips down to lightly brush against mine. "No, there's not. You still want to help me out of this suit?"

I go on my toes, pushing my mouth into his, more than ready to make this particular fantasy a reality. The fantasy of Logan and me, and the fantasy that started spinning in my head the second I saw him at the holiday party this afternoon. And I'm not about to waste this opportunity. I'm totally hot for Santa and dying for what comes next.

"I thought you'd never ask."

Logan grins against my lips, his hands trailing down my sides.

"I can't believe I'm asking now," he murmurs.

I pull back and laugh. "Honestly? Me neither." I run a finger down the fur that runs the length of his hard chest and stomach. "Especially since you made me turn away while you put that shirt on."

His lips tilt into a smirk. "Knowing what I know now, I can't believe you didn't peek."

I look up at him. "I wanted to," I admit.

"Can I tell you a secret?" he asks huskily. I nod. "I wanted you to watch."

My mouth pops open and my eyes go wide as my insides flutter. I swallow hard. "Don't say things like that," I repeat my plea from earlier today.

His hands cup my face, his features settling into a mask of concern. "Too much?"

I shake my head lightly and peer up at him. "No. I just want to take this slow and enjoy every minute of it. But if you say things like that, this is going to go very, very fast."

His only answer is the raise of one thick brow. He's so sexy without even trying. And his only response is to slowly lower his face to mine.

Our lips touch lightly, his tongue sliding gently into my mouth. I groan as I pull myself into him, savoring his taste as he gently explores my mouth.

After a few minutes of slow kisses, my whole body is humming with energy. My mind unable to believe we're here. My heart bursting with anticipation.

I end the kiss, sliding my hands to rest on his chest. "If we do this, it's going to change everything."

Logan grins, his perfect white teeth peeking through his full lips. And without warning, he scoops me up into his arms. "I sure hope so."

He returns his mouth to mine as he carries me to the couch, then breaks off only to gently lay me down before sliding on top of me.

"You're not worried?" I press before he can return to kissing me senseless.

He pulls his head back a fraction and fixes me with a look. "I'm fucking thrilled, Evie. But if you're worried, we don't have to do anything. I'm happy to just be here with you. We can get to know each other. And I bet you haven't eaten since you got —"

With a grin at his obvious concern for me, I cut him off with a kiss. "I'm not worried. I just wanted to make sure."

Logan makes a low rumbling sound in his chest that sends heat shooting through my body. And then he kisses me.

It's different this time. Still sweet and respectful, but deep and full of heat. It sets my body into a simmer, like molten lava is churning beneath my skin. And the longer it goes on, the more I need him.

I slip my hand down the suit jacket, clumsily fumbling at the buttons, baring his chest. My hand explores freely, as if it has a mind of its own. And in short order I find myself pushing at the sleeves. He helps, leaning up to wriggle out. And he wasn't kidding, about the top at least. It's all he had on.

I peer up at him, examining every inch of his beautiful body. He's fit but not overly muscled, with a small patch of gray hair at his chest that trails down his tight abs to … I bite my lip as I think about where that trail leads.

"If you keep looking at me like that, this is going to go very, very fast," he teases.

My eyes flick guiltily to his and I feel myself blush. "Sorry. You're just … amazing."

"So are you, Evie."

I make to shake my head, but he's not having it. His mouth meets mine again, his hands exploring more fervently this time. He lifts me so he can remove my top, and the cool rush of air against my skin is a sudden alert that I'm shirtless. With my boss.

I fight the urge to cover my eyes. It's not because I'm embarrassed. I just can't believe this is real. And when

Logan's eyes darken at the sight of me, my body tensing deliciously in response, the feeling intensifies. We're really going to do this.

The heat between my legs increases at the thought and I shudder.

"I have had so many fantasies about seeing you just like this," Logan says, his voice low and sexy.

He reaches out a hand and traces from the dip at the base of my neck, down. He stops between my breasts and our gazes collide.

"And what happens next in those fantasies?" I prompt. Needing him to touch me.

One finger lazily travels over the white lace on my left breast. It finds the nipple, teasing it until it peaks under the fabric. He slowly repeats it on the other side.

"I give you the kind of pleasure you deserve, Evie," he says. "That's what."

I suck in a sharp breath. Abruptly, he pulls my bra cup down and drops his mouth to my nipple. His tongue darts out and traces a hot, wet circle before sinking onto it and sucking gently. I arch into him, pleasure spiking through me.

So, this is definitely happening.

My hands become desperate for him, sliding over his broad shoulders, down his muscled arms as he continues to alternate breasts, kneading and sucking me into a frenzy.

When I can't take it anymore, my hand moves down his center, under the waistband of his ridiculous outfit. And true to his word, he's not wearing any underwear. What he is wearing is a hard-on that promises to devastate me.

As I work my hand over his length, I tremble with anticipation. He groans into my breast as I work him. *That sound.* Holy hell. I need him to make that sound more.

I push him back until he stops laving my breast with his tongue and allows me to climb up in front of him. I waste no time, pulling at his pants. He huffs a short breath and tips his head back, lifting his hips to allow it.

But the sight of his cock springing free is too much. My lust-fogged brain has no room for doubts anymore, no room for recognizing that I'm about to suck my boss's dick and that *that* is definitely going to change everything.

Instead, my mouth descends hungrily, wrapping around his thickness. The taste drives me just as crazy as his kiss. Salty and earthy and so male it hurts, but in the best way.

I suck him long and slow with just my mouth, my hands coming to rest on his massive thighs. He scoops my hair up with both hands and holds it behind my head.

I peer up at him just once to find him looking through half-closed lids, clearly as gone to this as I am, before drawing him in deeper, working him firmly with my mouth. A long groan escapes him, and it's everything I wanted.

"God, Evie, you're unbelievable," he moans.

I slide him out of my mouth and look up with a grin as I continue to work him with one hand. He smiles back down at me, the corners of his eyes crinkling. And it hits me right in the heart. I've known Logan for years. I know all about his family. Where he grew up. What his favorite foods are. But knowing him like this? I'd been longing for it more than I realized.

"Lay down," he says gently, breaking into my thoughts.

My eyes flick back up to his. I work my hand over him once, hard, before letting go. He shakes his head and laughs as I lay down languidly.

His strong hands pull at my leggings and panties until they've joined all of our other clothes on the floor. His hands travel back up my legs before he grasps under my knees and pulls my legs up. His eyes travel over my center greedily and I whimper knowing what he's about to do.

His gaze meets mine at the small noise. "You're beautiful," he assures me. "And I've dreamed about doing this."

And with that he's between my thighs, his tongue swirling over my clitoris, his thumb testing my entrance. I fight the urge to wriggle under the sudden intensity of feeling, closing my eyes and focusing on how damn fantastic he is at what he's doing.

His thumb teases me for a bit before he slides in a finger. It twists and turns inside my wet heat as it seeks its target. And when it finds it, it curls and strokes as his tongue spears against my clitoris. And the orgasm bursts out of me in pants and moans before I can stop it. Stars pop in my eyes as Logan rears up. I feel him seat himself at my entrance.

I breathe deep to steady myself and open my eyes. Looking down I can see he's already somehow gotten a condom on. I smirk up at him to tease him about his ninja condom skills, but the look on his face makes the words die on my tongue.

Knowing each other so long, I thought I'd seen all the faces of Logan. Happy. Angry. Amused. Contemplative. And a million more. But this? This expression undoes me. He's staring at me like I'm the most beautiful woman in the world. Like all he wants is me. And my heart sings.

I also realize he's waiting for my permission. I blink hard against the emotion and give a nod. And Logan enters me. Deliciously. Slowly. Perfectly.

He watches me as I lose the fight against the arch of my body. I watch him as he grits his teeth against the feel of me around him. Once he's fully in, his hands slide to my hips, tilting me as he leans in and kisses me softly.

He echoes the softness of his kiss with the first tilt of his hips, drawing slowly out before gliding gently back in. I nod in encouragement, wrapping my arms around his neck, my legs around his backside. I need this. I need him. I need more.

He continues to match kisses and thrusts until I'm panting, and my next orgasm is threatening to take me. But the slowness keeps it at bay, pushing the intensity to new levels.

"Please," I breathe. "More."

A slow smile spreads over Logan's face. "Anything for you, Evie." His hips pick up speed, but only slightly. My frown of frustration is met by a cheeky grin. "Say my name, baby."

I tighten around him at the words. So that's how he likes it? I grin back.

"Oh, Santa," I groan ostentatiously, grinding my hips against his.

His head drops into my chest as he laughs, his pace stuttering. I smile against his hair.

He looks back up, still chuckling. "Okay, I should've seen that coming," he allows, then places a soft, sultry kiss on my lips. "But you just landed yourself on the naughty list for that one."

"Oh no," I say in mock sadness.

He flicks an eyebrow. "Don't worry. My naughty girl is going to get exactly what she deserves."

He circles his hips before plunging back into me, this time not as softly. And he does it again, harder still. And faster. My breath hitches as my orgasm nears. But he doesn't stop, going harder and faster with each swing of his hips.

"Yes," I encourage him as I approach the edge.

"You like that?"

I nod. So he goes harder. Faster. It only takes two more thrusts, and this time I'm screaming his name for real as I topple over the edge into the mind-numbing bliss of my climax. As I fall, I hear Logan fall with me.

"Fuck, Evie," he groans, his mouth capturing mine in a brief yet crazy intense kiss. "That was phenomenal."

I sigh with contentment. "I should've gotten on the naughty list ages ago," I say in agreement.

Logan laughs. "And I should've dressed up like Santa ages ago."

"It wasn't the Santa costume," I assure him, reaching a hand up to touch his face. "It's always been you, Logan."

A small, desperate-sounding noise escapes him. "God, Evie, and it's always been you. Always." He kisses me then, and it feels like more than post-orgasmic reveling. It feels like the start of something big.

"Stay," I say when he breaks away. "Please?"

He smirks down at me. "Did you really think you were going to get rid of me after that?" He slowly withdraws, leaning back on his haunches. "Come on. Let's go take a shower."

On the surface it seems like an innocent and natural

suggestion. But something about his tone and the glint in his eye tells me he has much more than a shower planned.

And I'm here for it. Because he was just a dream for so long, and as difficult as it is to accept this new reality, I'm not standing in my own way anymore. I deserve to see where this goes. We deserve it.

LOGAN DOESN'T SPEND JUST THE NIGHT, HE PRETTY MUCH spends the entire break with me, alternating between our apartments. We only separated for our respective family functions — it's way too soon for doing those as a couple — and then reconnected for all those dates he promised and so much more. Including ringing in the New Year by making love. It left me hoping we get to do that for the rest of the year. Maybe more. Because my feelings for Logan have grown stronger quickly.

But now it's the Sunday before we go back to work, and reality is starting to set in. Especially since we haven't so much as mentioned work — well in a "what's going to happen next" kind of way — since that first night.

As we enjoy a late we've-been-in-bed-all-morning meal at my breakfast bar, I'm trying to figure out how to broach the subject when he beats me to it.

"So, I scheduled a meeting with Mark first thing tomorrow," he says.

My eyebrows jump. Mark Dubois is his boss, the second level manager of our department.

"Oh? What for?" I ask innocently, taking a sip of orange juice.

Logan turns his stool to face me, then hauls mine around so I'm facing him.

"I'm going to tell him that we've started dating. I thought about just trying to keep things between us until we figured out …" He trails off, biting into his lip.

"If this was really anything? It's okay to say it," I respond plainly.

He huffs a small laughs and nods. "Exactly. Except, the more time we spend together, the more I'm sure."

My heart races and I fidget in my chair. "Of what?"

He smiles and reaches for me, his hand settling against my neck, his thumb stroking along my jaw. "I was in love with you before that party, Evie. And I know that's probably a huge thing to drop on you so quickly. I thought at first I was being stupid, that maybe it was just the idea of you when I couldn't have you. But it's not. Every minute with you has made me realize that what I felt before is nothing compared to how I feel now, really being with you."

I close my eyes, my cheek dipping into his hand. When I reopen them, he's watching me nervously.

"I feel the exact same way," I assure him.

His shoulders drop with relief, a smiling breaking over his face. "Really?"

And this confident, intelligent, gorgeous man sounding so vulnerable undoes me. "Yes, really. I love you, Logan. And I think we should do what we have to do at work so we don't have to hide being together. I can move departments too. Whatever they want."

The suddenness and ferocity with which he moves forward and kisses me is startling. And then dazzling, as I melt into the fervency of his lips.

He finally breaks the kiss, leaning his forehead against mine. "I love you too. You have no idea how fucking happy I am to hear you say that."

"Then why don't you show me?" I whisper with a sly grin.

With a tilt of one eyebrow, he slides to his knees in front of me. "Good thing I wasn't quite done eating."

I bite into my lip as his hand slips under the oversized shirt I'm wearing and beneath the small strip of silk covering my sex. He strokes a finger through my wetness.

"And probably best I get this out of my system here," he says as his other hand bunches my shirt up.

I let out a laugh that's cut off by his tongue on me. I tilt my hips forward toward his waiting mouth.

"I hope you never get it out of your system," I admit, groaning as he works me.

I feel his laugh against my pussy. "Don't worry, I could do this forever."

My eyes go wide, and my hand grasps the hair at the back of his neck. He looks up at me and our gazes lock.

"Don't say things like that," I whisper.

"Even if I mean them?" he asks tenderly.

My heart hammers in my chest, my throat thick with emotion. And for once, I'm speechless. But strangely not because I'm scared. It should be insane to be talking about forever right now.

But then, when you know, you know. And I wasn't lying to him. For me, it's always been Logan. Maybe I just never let myself believe it ever could be always Logan. That he'd choose me too. I swallow hard.

"Because I do," he continues, rising so he's looking down into my eyes, running a hand down my cheek. "But for now, we can take this one day at a time if that's easier for you."

I hook a leg around him, so he has to dip down to get closer. "I've already told you. It's always been you."

He looks back at me just as intently as I'm looking at him. And he nods. His lips meet mine. His hand hitches my other leg up around him, sliding me to the edge of my seat, then frees his cock from his sweatpants. And we seal the promise in flesh as he slips inside of me.

This time is different. It's like he's worshipping me and claiming me all at once. I allow it. Because I was already his. And now he's mine, with the hope of forever.

HAPPY HOLIDAYS!

Want more? Check out Melanie A. Smith's latest release *Finding His Redemption: An Enemies to Lovers Rock Star Romance* at https://melanieasmithauthor.com/books-finding-his-redemption.html

Sign up for Melanie A. Smith's newsletter to get a FREE book plus all the latest news and more https://mailchi.mp/melanieasmithauthor.com/nlsignup

A NOTE FROM THE AUTHOR

Thank you so much for reading! Now … I need your help! Will you please take a minute to leave a review? It doesn't have to be long — just a couple sentences saying what you thought of the book on any retailer, goodreads, and/or BookBub. Your opinion is important to me, and for potential readers. Thank you!

ABOUT THE AUTHOR

Melanie A. Smith is an award-winning and international best-selling author of steamy contemporary romance fiction. A voracious reader and lifelong writer, Melanie's writing began at a young age with short stories and poetry. After college and a career as an aircraft engineer, she shifted to domestic engineering and property management and eventually found a balance where she was able to return to writing fiction. Melanie is also a Mensan and enjoys spending time with her family, cooking, and driving with the windows down and the stereo cranked up loud.